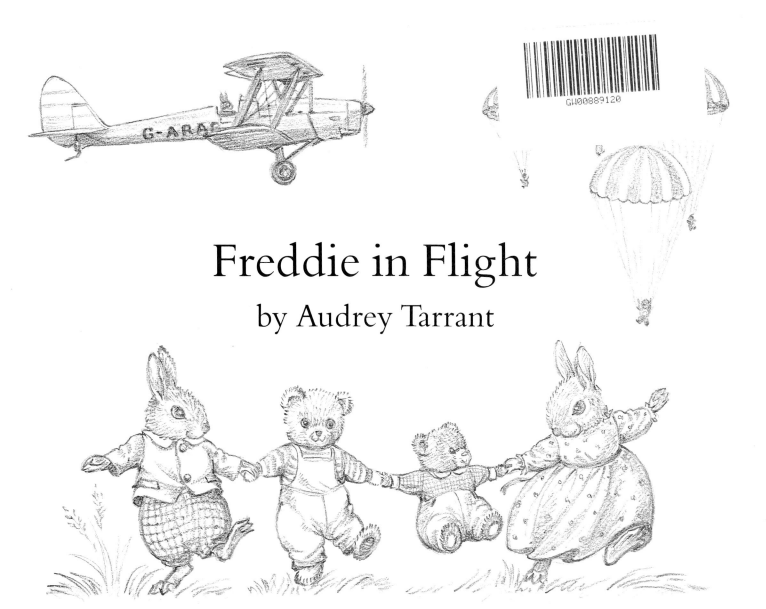

Freddie in Flight

by Audrey Tarrant

Printed in England. ISBN 0 85503 168 9

Rachel and her brothers, Paul, Stephen and Bryan, had gone out for the day to an Air Show. Rachel wanted to take Freddie the Teddy with her, but Mummy said he might get lost. So Freddie and Ted, Bryan's little teddy, were left sitting on the garden seat.

'It's so boring, just sitting here,' sighed Ted. Freddie looked up as an aeroplane zoomed low over the garden. Suddenly he jumped off the seat.

'Come on, Ted,' he said, 'we WON'T just sit here all day. Let's go into the wood and see if Bobbin and Belinda will play with us.' They ran to the bottom of the garden, crawled through a gap in the hedge and crossed the field to the duckpond. They stopped to say hello to Dilly and Dally, the ducks, and then went on into the wood.

As they ran down the path to the rabbits' house, they saw Bobbin and Belinda playing cricket. Bobbin hit the ball hard and Freddie, running quickly, caught it. 'HOWZAT!' cried Freddie.

Mrs Rabbit was packing up a picnic lunch for Bobbin and Belinda, who were going to another airfield for the day.

'Uncle Henry has an aeroplane there,' said Belinda, 'and sometimes he takes us flying.'

'We are learning to make parachute jumps too!' said Bobbin.

'Perhaps Freddie and Ted would like to go with you,' suggested Mrs Rabbit. Freddie and Ted shouted for joy.

Mr Rabbit, who was a train driver on the Woodland Railway, was just going off to the station. 'Get in the car, all of you,' he said, 'and I will drop you off at the airfield on my way.'

The two rabbits and the two teddy bears were so excited that they squeaked and chattered loudly as they bounced up and down in the back of the car.

'What a noise!' said Mr Rabbit and laughed, 'I'm glad it is not far to the airfield.' When Mr Rabbit stopped they tumbled out of the car, waved goodbye and ran on to the airfield.

'There's Uncle Henry working on his aeroplane in front of the hangar,' said Belinda. Uncle Henry was pleased to see them all as he needed lots of help. 'I'm giving the plane a thorough check and a good clean,' he said, 'so it's lucky you have brought Freddie and Ted with you today. Come with me and I will show you where everything is.'

Ted nudged Freddie and whispered, 'This is much better than going to the Air Show!'

Soon they were all very busy. Uncle Henry did the important work of making sure the aeroplane was safe to fly. Ted had the hose and washed the body and the wings, while Bobbin and Belinda dried and polished them. Freddie washed the wheels.

'OUCH!' squeaked Ted, as he knocked his elbow and dropped the nozzle of the hose.

'OUCH!' squeaked Freddie even louder, as the hose swung under the wing and squirted him with water.

'Ooh Freddie, I am so sorry,' gasped Ted as he rubbed his elbow. 'That's all right,' said Freddie, grinning, 'I was hot, and that has made me nice and cool.'

'We'll stop for lunch now,' said Uncle Henry, 'then you will soon dry off in the sun.' They went to the edge of the airfield and sat among the buttercups. It was a scrumptious picnic!

The aeroplane was ready to fly, but Uncle Henry could not find his goggles.

'What D I D I do with them?' he wondered. They searched in the aeroplane and under it, inside and outside the hangar, but N O goggles. Then Ted remembered that Uncle Henry's lunch had been in the bag with his flying kit and that the bag had been knocked over. Perhaps the goggles had fallen out? Freddie and Ted ran back across the field and searched in the long grass.

'I've got them,' shouted Ted.

Uncle Henry said that Freddie and Ted had been such a help that he would treat them to a flight. Freddie climbed up, but Ted suddenly felt frightened and would not go. Bobbin fetched a cushion for Freddie to sit on. Belts on! The engine roared, the propeller whirled, they bumped over the grass, they were O F F!

It was WONDERFUL! The aeroplane's nose tipped up and Freddie saw only the sky. The nose tipped steeply down, and the fields and trees rushed to meet him. 'OOPS!' gulped Freddie, and clutched his tummy. The aeroplane tipped sideways and the houses seemed to swing up beside him.

'There is our house with the duckpond next to it,' squeaked Freddie, 'and there is Mr Rabbit's steam engine coming out of the tunnel.'

Then Uncle Henry said, 'Now Freddie, YOU are going to fly the aeroplane.' Freddie gasped, and then did everything Uncle Henry told him to do. The aeroplane climbed up towards the clouds and then dived slowly down again. It turned to the right and rolled to the left. It went everywhere Freddie wanted it to go.

All too soon it was over, and they landed back on the airfield.

Ted felt a little bit sad when he heard what he had missed. He had been silly not to go with Freddie, but perhaps one day he would have another chance.

'Now we must go for our parachute jump lesson,' said Bobbin, who had been watching a parachutist land. They went to the other side of the field and met Mr Squirrel. He said he would teach Freddie and Ted too, and they had fun jumping off a box into the sandpit. They learned how to roll over so that they would not hurt themselves when they landed. He showed them how to put on their parachutes.

'I wish we could have a real jump,' said Ted.

'Ye-es,' said Freddie slowly. He was not QUITE sure if he would really enjoy it or not. 'I don't suppose we shall *ever* have a chance to try anyway.'

'Now it's time to stop for tea,' said Mr Squirrel, and Freddie and Ted suddenly knew it was LATE. They were so far from home, and it would take ages to walk back. Ted thought of his short little legs, and wondered if he COULD walk all that way.

'You have learnt so quickly that I will fly you home, and you can parachute into the field beside your house,' said Mr Squirrel.

They put on their parachutes and helmets, and climbed into the aeroplane with Mr Squirrel. Uncle Henry came to say goodbye to them and to watch them go.

'Goodbye, Uncle Henry, thank you for a lovely day,' they cried.

'Come and see me again soon,' he said.

'We WILL!' and Ted thought, 'So I AM going to fly after all!'

Freddie stood at the open door and thought, 'I'm NOT frightened . . . not really.' Then he heard Mr Squirrel say, 'Jump, Freddie,' and, remembering all he had been taught, he took a deep breath and jumped. Ted stood at the door and thought 'I'M not frightened,' swallowed hard and jumped too.

'ONE, TWO, THREE,' counted Freddie and then, with a jerk, his parachute opened and he floated slowly down. Already he could see the house with the field next to it, and Dilly and Dally swimming on the pond. With a loud quacking, Dilly and Dally flew up as they saw the four parachutes coming down towards them.

'Hallo,' shouted Freddie, 'look, I can fly too!'

'Not as fast as we can,' quacked Dilly, as they flew round him and then down to the pond again.

As Freddie floated nearer to the ground, a gust of wind caught his parachute and took him over the pond.

'Oh NO!' he squeaked, 'I'm going to get wet again.' But he remembered which parachute cord to pull and steered away from the pond.

'That was a near miss,' quacked Dally, 'perhaps you ought to learn to swim next!'

Soon Ted, Bobbin and Belinda had landed safely too. 'We've done it,' said Ted, as they took off their parachutes, 'and wasn't it fun, Freddie!'

Bobbin and Belinda picked up the four parachutes to take home with them. They told Freddie and Ted to leave their helmets under the hedge – they would come back for those later.

'Goodbye Bobbin, goodbye Belinda, thank you for a marvellous day,' called Freddie and Ted, as they ran towards the gap in the hedge.

Just as Freddie and Ted clambered up onto the garden seat, they heard the car come back. Then they heard running footsteps, and Rachel and Bryan picked them up.

'Oh Freddie,' said Rachel, 'what a shame you had to miss the Air Show. You WOULD have enjoyed watching the planes.'

'And we even saw parachutists too,' said Bryan.

Freddie and Ted grinned at each other. If only Rachel and Bryan knew! THEY had FLOWN in an aeroplane, and THEY had PARACHUTED too!